Dusty Crophopper is an aeroplane with a very big problem – he's afraid of heights! To find out what happens when Dusty enters a high-flying race, you can read along with me in your book. You will know it's time to turn the page when you hear this sound ...
Let's begin now.

Narrator: David Jeremiah
Dusty Crophopper: Dane Cook
Leadbottom: Cedric the Entertainer
Chug: Brad Garrett
Skipper: Stacy Keach
Roper: Sinbad
Bulldog: John Cleese
El Chupacabra: Carlos Alazraqui
Ripslinger: Roger Craig Smith
Dottie: Teri Hatcher

Producers: Ted Kryczko & Jeff Sheridan
Executive Producer: Randy Thornton

Walt Disney RECORDS

℗ 2013 Walt Disney Records
© 2013 Disney Enterprises, Inc.

This edition published by Parragon Books Ltd in 2013

Parragon Books Ltd
Chartist House
15–17 Trim Street
Bath BA1 1HA, UK
www.parragon.com

ISBN 978-1-4454-9678-8

Printed in China

Bath · New York · Singapore · Hong Kong · Cologne · Delhi
Melbourne · Amsterdam · Johannesburg · Shenzhen

Dusty Crophopper was a small-town crop duster with a big dream. More than anything he wanted to race in the Wings Around The Globe Rally.

Whenever Dusty closed his eyes he would picture himself as a world-class racer. He dreamed he could even fly faster than the quickest jet planes.

But for now, reality stood between Dusty and his dream. Dusty's boss, Leadbottom, wanted Dusty to focus on his job instead. "Pay attention! You're daydreaming again!"

Dusty tried to explain. "Look, I am more than just a crop duster...."

Leadbottom didn't understand why Dusty would rather race than spray crops. "You ask me, more racers should want to be crop dusters."

But that didn't stop Dusty from thinking about the Wings Around The Globe Rally while he was working.

Dusty's best friend, Chug the fuel truck, wanted to help make Dusty's dream come true. When Dusty finished spraying the crops, he met Chug at a field outside Propwash Junction.

There, Chug helped Dusty train for the rally's qualifying race. "Okay, now let's try some treeline moguls. C'mon. All the way up and down...."

Even with Chug's directions Dusty needed to go faster if he wanted to get into the rally. So Chug suggested a coach with some flying experience. "My buddy Sparky says the Skipper was a legendary flight instructor in the navy."

Skipper had been a hero in the Jolly Wrenches flying squad. Even though he hadn't flown in years, everyone still talked about his daring missions.

Dusty wasn't sure what Skipper would say when he asked for help. "I was wondering if you would ... train me?"

Skipper wasn't interested. "Go home. You're in over your head, kid!"

Even without Skipper's help, Dusty was determined to try out for the Wings Around The Globe Rally. When it was his turn at the qualifying race Dusty flew better than he ever had before.

But Dusty wasn't quite fast enough to qualify for the big race. Another plane beat Dusty by just a fraction of a second.

That night, one of the race officials visited Propwash Junction. He said that another racer had been disqualified for cheating.

Chug cheered. "He's in! Dusty's in the race!"

Dusty wanted to celebrate with his friends, but a big secret was troubling him.

After hearing the news, Skipper changed his mind about training Dusty. "You want speed, right? Then look up! The Highway in the Sky. Tailwinds like nothing you've ever flown."

Dusty glanced at the cloud streets overhead. They seemed high ... really high. He shut his eyes and flew as far up as he could. But when Dusty opened his eyes, everything started to spin.

Dusty knew he had to tell Skipper the truth. "I'm afraid of heights!"

"Scared of heights and you want to race around the world?" Skipper was shocked, but he decided he could work around Dusty's problem.

Skipper taught Dusty to race the shadows of high-flying planes. That way, Dusty could stay close to the ground.

Little by little, the crop duster started flying faster
and faster. When he finally won against a shadow,
Skipper smiled. "He's ready."

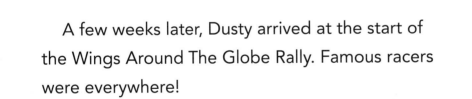

A few weeks later, Dusty arrived at the start of
the Wings Around The Globe Rally. Famous racers
were everywhere!

Right away, Dusty met one of his heroes. "Wow!
Bulldog, from the European Cup!"

But Bulldog didn't seem very friendly. "I don't know
how things work in the backwater from which
you hail, matey, but this is a competition.
Every plane for himself."

The race hadn't even started, and Dusty was already
missing his friends from home.

Then Dusty met some of the other planes.

One racer, El Chupacabra, wanted to make a big entrance. "*Atención, señors y señoritas!* The hero of the people has arrived!"

Dusty was in awe. "He's the indoor racing champion of all Mexico!"

El Chu was thrilled that Dusty knew who he was.
"We will have many adventures, you and I! I will see
you in the skies, *amigo*!"

At last, it was time for the first part of the race to begin. The planes lined up on the runways and prepared for take-off. Then one of the judges dropped the flag.

The racers zoomed into the sky. But while the other planes climbed higher and higher, Dusty flew as low as he could, just above the Atlantic Ocean. Dusty was pelted with stinging snow and frosty chunks of ice! When he finally landed in Iceland, he was in last place.

Dusty wasn't the only plane having trouble, though.
On the next leg of the race Bulldog sent out a call for
help. "Mayday! Mayday! Mayday! I'm blinded."

Bulldog was leaking oil – and losing altitude fast.
If someone didn't help, Bulldog could crash!

Dusty zoomed over to Bulldog. "Apply your left aileron. Stop roll. Now quick, pull up!"

Bulldog did everything Dusty said, even though he couldn't see where he was flying. "Are you still there?"

Dusty replied at once. "I'm right here. I'll fly right alongside you." Dusty guided Bulldog to a safe landing in Germany.

"Thanks for your help, matey." Bulldog didn't understand why Dusty had slowed down to help him, but he was still grateful.

As the race continued Dusty pulled out of last place ... and got some fans of his very own! Everyone loved cheering for the underdog crop duster.

But one plane wasn't very happy about Dusty's success – a champion racer named Ripslinger. "Why are they wasting their time with him? He's a tractor with wings!"

Ripslinger thought that crop dusters shouldn't compete with real racing planes.

With just two legs left in the race, Dusty moved into second place!

The next flight, across the Pacific Ocean, would be long and dangerous. Before the race Dusty radioed his friends back in Propwash Junction. Skipper was especially worried. "Be careful."

Before they hung up, Chug had something
exciting to tell Dusty. "We're going to meet you
in Mexico!"

Dusty could hardly believe it! "Really?"

But on the way to Mexico, one of Ripslinger's teammates broke Dusty's navigation antenna! Dusty flew for miles in the wrong direction.

He was about to run out of gas when two navy jets, Bravo and Echo, approached.

Dusty asked them for help. "I'm running on vapours. I-I need to land!"

Thanks to Bravo and Echo, Dusty made a safe landing on the *Dwight D. Flysenhower* – Skipper's old ship!

On board, Dusty saw the Jolly Wrenches Wall of Fame, which showed that Skipper had only flown one mission. Dusty was sure it was a mistake.

As Dusty flew to Mexico he got caught in a terrible storm. The wind battered against him, damaging everything from his landing gear to his wings.

When Dusty finally arrived in Mexico, his worried friends surrounded him. But Dusty wanted to talk to Skipper right away. "One mission?"

Skipper told Dusty the truth about his first mission. His team had been in a horrible battle – Skipper had lost many of his friends. "After that ... I just couldn't bring myself to fly again."

Dusty didn't know what to say, so he just turned and rolled away.

With so many broken parts, Dusty was ready
to give up.

Dottie the mechanic urged him to keep going.
"You're a racer. And now the whole world knows it."

Then the other racers rolled into the hangar.
Each one brought new parts for Dusty!

El Chu gave him a pair of wings. "*Amigo*, I cannot
bear the thought of competing without you."

Even Bulldog brought Dusty a new satellite
navigational system! "In case you ever find yourself
lost ... without a friend to help you through it."

Dusty was very grateful.

With all the new parts, Dusty began the last leg of the race. Everyone was thrilled that Dusty was back ... except for Ripslinger. "Bolting on a few new parts doesn't change who you are."

Ripslinger's goons started ramming into Dusty to make him crash. Dusty thought he was done for – until Skipper came flying over to help! After so many years on the ground Skipper took to the air just when Dusty needed him the most. "Go get 'em!"

Dusty caught up to Ripslinger, but he couldn't go fast enough to pass the champion plane.

Dusty looked up and saw a fast cloud street overhead. "Don't look down. Don't look down." Taking a deep breath, he flew higher and higher. "Oh, yeah! *Whooo-hoooo!*"

As Ripslinger approached the finish line he had no idea that Dusty was soaring above him. Ripslinger was sure that he would win. He even turned to smile at the cameras. "Get my good side, fellas!"

At the last second, Dusty zoomed past Ripslinger – and won the race! The whole world celebrated, especially the gang from Propwash Junction. Dusty had conquered his fear of heights and now his high-flying adventures were just beginning!